American Indian Nations

The
Comanche
Nomads of the Southern Plains

by Mary Englar

Capstone *press*
Mankato, Minnesota

Capstone Press
151 Good Counsel Drive, P.O. Box 669, Mankato, Minnesota 56002
http://www.capstone-press.com

Library of Congress Cataloging-in-Publication Data
Englar, Mary.
 The Comanche: Nomads of the southern plains/by Mary Englar.
  v. cm.—(American Indian nations)
 Includes bibliographical references and index.
 Contents: Who are the Comanche?—Traditional life—Americans bring
change—The Comanche today—Sharing the traditions
  map: The Comanche past and present—Recipe: Comanche plum bars.
 ISBN 0-7368-2180-5 (hardcover)
 1. Comanche Indians—Juvenile literature. [1. Comanche Indians.
2. Indians of North America—Southwest, New. 3. Indians of North
America—Great Plains.] I. Title. II. Series.
E99.C85E64 2004
978.004'9745—dc21   2002156008

Summary: Provides an overview of the past and present Comanche people.
Traces their customs, family life, history, and culture, as well as relations with
the U.S. government.

Editorial Credits

Charles Pederson, editor; Kia Adams, series designer; Molly Nei, book
designer and illustrator; Kelly Garvin, photo researcher; Karen Risch,
product planning editor

Photo Credits

Cover images: Comanche tepee on the plains, Marilyn "Angel" Wynn; Comanche
cradleboard, Denver Public Library

Americans for Indian Opportunity, 43; Art Resource/Smithsonian American Art
Museum, Washington, D.C., 8–9, 18–19, 20; Art Resource/National Museum of
American Art, Washington, D.C., 24; Capstone Press/Gary Sundermeyer, 15;
Comanche Language and Cultural Preservation Committee/photo courtesy of
Barbara and Kenneth Goodin, 35; Corbis/Bettmann, 30; Comanche Moon by Frank
McCarthy, The Greenwich Workshop Inc., www.greenwichworkshop.com, 22–23;
Digital Vision, 14–15; Kansas State Historical Society, 27; Library of Congress, 29;
Marilyn "Angel" Wynn, 4, 32, 36, 37, 38, 40, 44, 45; National Archives, 12; North
Wind Picture Archives, 17; Stock Montage Inc./Newberry Library, 11

Capstone Press wishes to thank Annie Ross, Ph.D., of the University
of California-Davis Native American Studies Department for her
assistance in preparing this book.

1 2 3 4 5 6 08 07 06 05 04 03

Table of Contents

Features

A Comanche leader proudly wears a Comanche headdress. Today's Comanche are descendants of a people known as the Lords of the Plains.

Chapter One

Who Are the Comanche?

The Comanche (kuh-MAN-chee) are an
American Indian nation who once were
called the Lords of the Plains. The
Comanche have several other names.
The name Comanche comes from the Ute
Indian word "komantcia." It means enemy
or always ready to fight. The Spanish
adopted the word, and it later became
Comanche in English. The Comanche call
themselves "Numunuh." This word means
the people.

In the 1600s, the Comanche moved
from present-day Wyoming and Idaho
to the edge of the Rocky Mountains. When
the Comanche left the mountains about

1700, they moved onto the Great Plains. These flat grasslands stretch from the Rocky Mountains to the Mississippi River. The plains were dry and hot in summer and cold and windy in winter. The plains were also home to large herds of buffalo.

The Comanche hunted buffalo for most of their food. They moved often from place to place while following the herds. The Comanche camped near the buffalo at campsites with good sources of water and with grass for their horses. This area where they lived and hunted for food on the southern plains is often called "Comancheria."

Over the years, the Comanche have lived in many places. By the late 1700s, they lived in parts of present-day Colorado, Kansas, New Mexico, Oklahoma, and Texas. Today, many live in southwestern Oklahoma and other states.

According to the 2000 U.S. Census, 10,120 people are Comanche. Many Comanche live in Oklahoma, Texas, California, and other states. About half the Comanche live near their government headquarters in Lawton, Oklahoma.

The Comanche work in many professions. Some are doctors, lawyers, teachers, nurses, writers, and artists. Others lease their land to cattle ranchers and oil companies.

The Comanche were once one of the most powerful Indian nations on the Great Plains. Today, they continue to protect and promote their history, language, and culture.

The Comanche Past and Present

Legend

/// Comanche Hunting Lands in the 1700s

Modern Comanche Lands

Modern United States

Great Plains

Mexico

COLORADO

KANSAS

NEW MEXICO

OKLAHOMA

TEXAS

MEXICO

Gulf of Mexico

N
W E
S

Scale
Miles
0   62.5   125
0   50   100
Kilometers

Some American Indian tribes lived in tepees on the Great Plains. The Comanche tanned buffalo hides to cover their tepees.

Chapter Two

Traditional Life

The Comanche were nomads for hundreds of years. They moved often to follow large herds of buffalo. The Comanche lived in small groups called bands. Each band usually made its own camp. Most camps were only a few tentlike shelters called tepees, but some camps had many tepees.

The Comanche picked campsites that were close to streams. Their campsites had grass for their horses and wood for fires. They hunted antelope, deer, or buffalo for food.

When a band leader decided his band should move, the women packed the belongings. They took the tepees down.

The women made a sledlike device of tepee poles and buffalo skins called a travois. They tied the poles to the sides of a horse or mule. Buffalo skins stretched between the poles carried food, clothing, and other belongings. The travois dragged along the ground behind the animal.

The Comanche lived in small, single-family bands and larger bands made up of several related families. Comanche people sometimes moved from one band to live with a different band. Each band welcomed new members.

The bands shared a strong sense of community, but no band could speak for another. One Comanche band might agree to trade peacefully or to stop raiding traders' villages. At the same time, another band might attack the villages.

The Importance of Buffalo

The Comanche needed buffalo for clothing, tools, and food. The people used nearly every part of the buffalo. The women used leather from buffalo skins to make clothing and tepees. The buffalo's stomach could carry water. The bones, hooves, and horns made good cups and spoons. Sinew from the buffalo's back was used to sew skins together. This tough body tissue was also used to string bows. The Comanche ate most of the buffalo meat. The women left only the buffalo heart because they believed it would bring more buffalo when needed.

The Comanche usually hunted buffalo in the summer and fall. In summer, the buffalo had lost their winter fur. The remaining fur clung tightly to the skin, making the skins good for trading or for tepees and clothing. In late fall, the buffalo's heavy winter fur was good for warm winter clothing.

Buffalo were important to the Comanche, who used almost every part of the animals.

The Comanche set up separate camps for buffalo hunts. The women built shelters. They set up wooden frames to hold buffalo meat while it dried. All healthy men, women, and older children moved to the hunting camp. Older adults, young children, and sick people remained at the main camp.

The Comanche were excellent hunters. They often needed only one arrow to kill a buffalo. Each hunter marked his

The women built wooden frames to dry buffalo meat in the sun. Women also set up tepees whenever their band moved to a new camp.

arrows. After a hunt, the marked arrows showed which man had killed which animal. That hunter received the meat from that animal. Some men gave extra meat to other families and to older people who had no hunters to feed them.

The Comanche used the meat in different ways. For days after the hunt, people ate fresh meat. They dried the rest for use in pemmican, a mixture of dried meat and crushed wild fruit or nuts. Pemmican could be stored for a year or more when well prepared.

Women's Roles

Comanche women did much of the work in camp. They sewed clothing and tepees, took care of young children, and prepared food. They carried water from streams and gathered firewood. Women set up and took down tepees when a band moved to a new campsite.

Women prepared a variety of foods. They cooked buffalo, antelope, elk, and deer. They picked wild plums, cherries, and grapes. They gathered wild potatoes, onions, radishes, mesquite beans, and other wild vegetables. Tree nuts, such as acorns and pecans, were another source of food.

At a young age, girls learned to prepare and use animal skins. Soaking, scraping, and softening the skins into leather took many days. When the skins were ready, the women cut the skins into pieces for leggings, moccasins, and dresses. They used sinew to sew the clothing together.

For the Comanche and other nomadic people, tepees were a practical shelter. Tepees were waterproof. They were warm in winter. They were light and easy to move.

Women made tepees. Prepared leather skins were taken to an expert tepee maker. This woman planned the tepee and gathered other women to sew together the skins. Some tepees had to be large enough to hold 20 people. Each tepee had between 10 and 17 buffalo skins stretched across a frame of straight poles.

Children

The Comanche valued their children. Having more people meant greater strength for the band.

For the first nine or 10 months after giving birth, mothers wrapped their babies in cloths and tied them into cradleboards. These boards allowed mothers to carry their children easily. The mothers could set aside the cradleboards, and babies could safely watch from the cradleboards as their mothers worked.

Comanche Plum Bars

The Comanche sometimes used wild berries and plums to sweeten foods. Today, the Comanche sometimes buy plums in stores when they cannot find wild ones. Plum bars are served at celebrations and special occasions.

Ingredients

2 cups (480 mL) water
1 cup (240 mL) dried, pitted plums
2 eggs
1 cup (240 mL) light brown sugar
½ cup (120 mL) buttermilk
1 teaspoon (5 mL) vanilla extract
2 cups (480 mL) all-purpose flour

¼ teaspoon (1.2 mL) salt
¼ teaspoon (1.2 mL) allspice
1 cup (240 mL) pecans, chopped
2 tablespoons (30 mL) powdered sugar

Equipment

nonstick cooking spray
9- by 13-inch (23-centimeter by 33-centimeter) baking pan
medium saucepan
liquid measuring cup
masher
medium mixing bowl

electric mixer
measuring spoons
dry-ingredient measuring cups
mixing spoon
oven mitts
cooling rack
spoon

What You Do

1. Preheat oven to 325°F (160°C). Use nonstick cooking spray to grease baking pan.
2. Pour water in saucepan and bring to boil. Reduce heat and add dried plums. Boil plums for 5 minutes. Drain water. Mash plums and set aside.
3. In medium mixing bowl, beat eggs. Mix in brown sugar, buttermilk, and vanilla. Add flour, salt, and allspice. Mix well. Stir in plums and pecans to form a batter.
4. Pour the batter into the baking pan. Spread the mixture evenly. Place pan in oven and bake for 35 to 40 minutes. Bars should be golden brown when done.
5. Use oven mitts to remove pan from oven. Place the pan on cooling rack. Let cool for 15 minutes.
6. Use a spoon to sprinkle powdered sugar on the bars.

Makes 32 bars

15

Children learned by watching and listening to adults. As soon as children could walk, they followed their mothers around camp. Girls were given dolls and learned to sew clothes for them. The girls also pretended to cook.

Boys and girls learned to ride as soon as they could sit on a horse and hold the reins. Children learned to ride at about age 4 or 5. The children spent most of their day on horseback.

Men's Roles

Comanche men taught the boys about hunting, history, and Comanche traditions. Boys began to learn about hunting around age 6. Fathers were often away hunting, so grandfathers made bows and arrows to teach the boys to hunt. Grandfathers taught the boys to ride and shoot. Grandfathers also taught young boys about Comanche beliefs.

As boys became older, they practiced for hours with their horses. They learned to pick up objects off the ground while riding full speed. They practiced picking up a person from the ground and swinging this person onto their horses. This skill was helpful when men rescued fellow warriors during fights. Boys learned to use their horses as shields. They shot arrows under the horses' necks while hanging from the horses' sides.

Horses

Horses have an important place in American Indian history. The Spanish used horses when they came to the American Southwest in the late 1500s. In 1680, Pueblo Indian attacks forced the Spanish to leave New Mexico. The Spanish left behind many horses. The Pueblo kept the horses. They began to trade horses to other Indians. The Comanche obtained horses about 1700. They quickly became famous horsemen of the Great Plains. By 1800, the use of horses had spread among Indians from the Southwest to the Rocky Mountains, Great Plains, and Canada.

Horses were valuable to the Comanche. They used horses to hunt buffalo, pull travois, and carry riders. A gift of horses was given to a bride. To get horses, the Comanche stole them or traded for them. Warriors also won horses in battle.

The more horses a Comanche man had, the wealthier he was. A skillful Comanche might own hundreds of horses. A leader might own thousands. Comanche leaders lent their extra horses to band members for moving camp, hunting buffalo, and fighting wars.

The Comanche respected their warriors. Young men earned the right to become warriors. They first had to prove their bravery while hunting. Successful hunters could join a war party at age 15 or 16. If a boy was a good warrior, he might be elected a war leader.

Religion

The Comanche believed nature was filled with powerful spirits. The people believed a man received power from these spirits. This power was called medicine.

When a young man was ready to act as an adult, he made a vision quest. This important event helped him find medicine to feed and protect his family.

The young man first visited a medicine man in camp for spiritual cleansing. The young man then took a pipe, a buffalo robe, tobacco, and a flint to light the pipe. He walked to a high hill or other lonely place. He sat alone

without eating for four days and nights. During those four days, the young man prayed, smoked the tobacco, and waited for a vision of a guardian spirit.

Young Indian warriors often practiced their hunting skills. The Comanche were famous horsemen of the Great Plains. One skill they learned was to shoot with their bow and arrows from under their horses' necks.

19

Hunting Dance

Before the hunters left the main camp on a buffalo hunt, they gathered in the evenings for a Hunting Dance. They danced to show happiness about hunting. The members of the band built a fire in the center of the camp. One man kept the fire going, and others brought firewood. Men began drumming and singing. Men and women lined up across from each other. When the music began, the women chose a partner from the men. Hunters often danced until about midnight and then went to sleep. The dance sometimes went on for several nights until the hunters left for the hunt.

The Comanche believed a guardian spirit gave the young man power. The spirit also gave him a set of rules. If a man did not have a vision the first time, he could try again another time.

Medicine was important to the Comanche. If a Comanche man followed the guardian spirits' rules, his medicine would be strong. Some men's medicine was so strong they could share it with others. Sharing their medicine made them more respected in the band. A woman could learn about a husband's power but she could not seek power on her own.

Marriage

Comanche marriages were not complicated. When a young man wanted to marry a young woman, he gave horses to her father or brother. The girl's family discussed the young man's skills as a hunter and warrior. If he gave many horses, it showed he was a skillful raider. The family could be sure he could provide food for his bride. If the family members accepted the offer, they added the horses to their herd. If the family refused, they returned the horses to the young man.

Most Comanche bands did not have a special marriage ceremony. A family sometimes prepared a feast to announce the marriage. Other times, the band leader might announce it to the band. Often, the new bride simply moved in with the young man and his relatives.

The Comanche sometimes captured horses during raids.

Chapter Three

Americans Bring Change

The Comanche moved from the Rocky Mountains to the southern Great Plains around 1700. They wanted more horses. The Spanish, who had settled in New Mexico, traded horses, food, metal tools, and cooking utensils for buffalo skins. The Comanche also raided Spanish villages to obtain horses. In 1786, the Spanish signed a peace agreement with the Comanche to stop the attacks.

The Comanche became major traders. They traded with the French in Louisiana for guns and bullets. They traded with other Plains Indians for beads, food, and tools.

When Americans settled in Texas and the Great Plains in the early 1800s, the Comanche also traded with them.

Fighting with Others

In 1821, American businessmen opened the Santa Fe Trail. This trade route from Missouri into New Mexico ran across northern Comanche territory. Fights along the trail between

American Indian nations fought each other for territory.

Americans and different Indian nations were common. The Comanche were the most powerful tribe on the southern Great Plains and often were blamed for the fights. Americans sometimes attacked the Comanche in revenge. Americans often believed the Comanche had taken part in the fights, even when they had not.

Fights also occurred between the Comanche and other Indians. During the 1820s and 1830s, the U.S. government began moving American Indians from the eastern United States to Kansas and the Indian Territory. Indian Territory later became Oklahoma. Some of these eastern Indians had to hunt for food in Comanche land. The Comanche fought to protect their hunting ground.

In 1835, the Comanche signed the Camp Holmes Treaty with the U.S. government. The Comanche promised to keep peace with the eastern Indian nations.

More and more Americans met the Comanche. In 1848, gold was discovered in California. Thousands of white Americans traveled through Comanche land to California hoping to become rich. Americans moving west carried diseases. In 1848, many Comanche died of smallpox. Cholera struck the Comanche in 1849. Comanche bodies could not fight these diseases. Between 1849 and 1851, about 8,000

Comanche died. The Comanche nation never regained full strength after these deaths.

When the U.S. Civil War (1861–1865) began, U.S. soldiers in the West were sent east to fight. These soldiers had protected settlers and U.S. businesses on the Great Plains. When the soldiers left, the plains lay open to the Indians.

By 1865, the Comanche were at war with the United States. They stopped wagons from traveling the Santa Fe Trail. The Comanche also forced settlers out of Texas and took back Comanche land.

Moving to the Reservation

After the Civil War, the U.S. Army returned west to control the Comanche and other Indians. In 1867, the U.S. government tried to make a final peace. Many of the Comanche, Kiowa, and Kiowa-Apache Indians signed the Medicine Lodge Treaty in Kansas. These groups agreed to leave their territory and live on a reservation in Indian Territory.

For years, soldiers fought to keep Indians on reservations. With the Indians on reservations, Americans could use the plains for ranching and farming.

The Comanche people were one group who did not always stay on their reservation. Nearly half the Comanche never lived on the reservation.

In 1874, the Comanche fought the Battle of Palo Duro Canyon in Texas. The Comanche had been fighting the U.S. Army and American buffalo hunters. The hunters were

Iron Mountain's Camp was a reservation home of the Comanche near Fort Sill, Indian Territory.

rapidly killing many buffalo. At Palo Duro Canyon, soldiers fought a large group of Comanche. Few Comanche were killed in the fighting, but the soldiers captured nearly 1,500 horses. The soldiers burned Comanche tepees and food. Without horses, shelter, or food, many Comanche returned to the reservation. There, they could get food and housing from the U.S. government.

Between 1865 and 1875, buffalo hunters killed more than 14 million buffalo. Killing buffalo destroyed the main food supply for Indians still living off the reservations. The killing of the buffalo herds forced most of the remaining Comanche onto the reservation.

The Kwahada Band of Comanche, or Kwahada, refused to move to the reservation. They stayed on their land in northern Texas. They continued to live as they wanted. They stole cattle from Texans and sold or traded them in New Mexico. They stole horses from the U.S. Army and from Texas ranchers and traded them to other Indians.

In mid-1875, Comanche leader Quanah Parker gave up the Kwahada Band of Comanche to the army. His surrender at Fort Sill, in present-day Oklahoma,

Quanah Parker (1850?–1911)

Quanah Parker was born to Peta Nacona and Cynthia Parker around 1850 in northern Texas. Quanah had one brother and one sister.

When Peta Nacona died in the 1860s, Quanah Parker took his place as the Kwahada war leader. When the other Comanche bands signed the Medicine Lodge Treaty in 1867, Parker's band did not. They attacked towns and forts. They tried to drive the buffalo hunters from the plains. After many battles, Parker and the Kwahada Band finally surrendered at Fort Sill in 1875.

Parker could speak English, Spanish, and Comanche. This skill helped him become a leader for the Comanche on the reservation. He wanted his people to go to school and learn to survive in new ways. He fought against the General Allotment Act of 1887. This law divided Indian reservations into small pieces. Parker traveled many times to Washington, D.C., to represent the Comanche. He promoted a religion that blended Christianity and ancient Indian traditions from Mexico. The religion became known as the Native American Church.

ended the fighting. His band joined the other Comanche on the Indian Territory reservation.

Allotment and Beyond

In 1887, the U.S. Congress passed the General Allotment Act. This law allowed the U.S. government

Quanah Parker (standing at right) and other Comanche leaders visited Washington, D.C. They wanted to challenge the General Allotment Act.

to take away most reservation land. Each Indian family was allowed to choose only 160 acres (65 hectares) of land to live on. All leftover reservation land was given or sold to white settlers. Parker and other Comanche leaders traveled to Washington, D.C., to challenge the law. They were unsuccessful. The Indians could choose their land, but they could not stop the allotment.

The Comanche reservation was divided into allotments. The Comanche lost more than two-thirds of their reservation land. In 1907, the Indian Territory became the state of Oklahoma.

Parker and other Comanche believed it was wise to stop fighting against the U.S. government. They decided to learn what they needed to survive in this new world. They went to school and became farmers. But they did not forget their Comanche ways.

No longer warriors of the plains, the Comanche became fighters in the U.S. Army. The Comanche first joined a company of army scouts at Fort Sill. Other Comanche later served the military in World War I (1914–1918) and World War II (1939–1945). Comanche soldiers have fought during the Korean War (1950–1953), the Vietnam War (1954–1975), and later conflicts. The Comanche respect and honor their people who serve in the military.

Modern Comanche gather to celebrate
their traditions at a veterans' dance.

Chapter Four

The Comanche Today

Before World War II, many Comanche farmed or ranched on allotment land near Lawton, in southwestern Oklahoma. Today, more than 60 percent of the Comanche live within 25 miles (40 kilometers) of Lawton. They work in farming, ranching, the oil industry, and many other professions. Other Comanche have left the area to find jobs or attend college.

Comanche Government

In 1967, the Comanche adopted a constitution and became recognized as the Comanche Nation of Oklahoma. A tribal council governs the Comanche. The council is made up of Comanche men who are age 18 or older. The members elect seven council members to serve for three-year terms on the Comanche Business Committee.

The business committee and tribal council manage Comanche educational and social programs. The programs include alcohol and drug treatment, home improvement programs, and health programs.

The Comanche work hard to protect their water and other natural resources. The Comanche Nation Office of Environmental Programs tests water quality in eight counties near Lawton. They test the water in rivers, lakes, and streams to make sure it is safe for people and wildlife. The Comanche work closely with the U.S. Environmental Protection Agency.

Education is important to the Comanche. They seek to keep their language alive by teaching it to their children. The tribal government also provides money for students to attend college or vocational training schools.

Comanche Code Talkers

In 1941, Comanche men joined the U.S. Army in World War II. Along with volunteers from other Indian nations, the men became known as code talkers. During their training, the Comanche created a 100-word code based on their language. Since the Comanche language had no words for tank or machine guns, the men used other Comanche words. The Comanche word for turtle meant tank. The Comanche word for sewing machine was used to mean machine guns.

In 1945, 14 Comanche code talkers landed with other U.S. soldiers at Normandy, France. The code talkers sent messages from the battlefield to headquarters. At headquarters, other Comanche translated the messages.

Years later, the code talkers were recognized for their war efforts. In 1989, the French government honored the surviving code talkers with the French National Order of Merit. In 1999, the U.S. government honored Charles Chibitty with the Knowlton Award. Chibitty was the last surviving Comanche code talker. He accepted the award for all the code talkers.

Continuing their Heritage

Yearly social events bring the Comanche home to visit friends and family. The Comanche Homecoming and the Comanche Nation Fair offer basketball and horseshoe competitions, dance competitions, and Comanche arts and crafts sales. The Comanche welcome these opportunities to share their culture with other people.

The Comanche consider themselves Americans, while they continue to remember their proud Comanche heritage. They learn the Comanche language. They prepare traditional foods. They perform the songs and dances of the Comanche people. They teach their children to continue the traditions the Comanche have practiced for hundreds of years.

Pemmican is a traditional Comanche food made from dried buffalo meat, fat, and crushed fruit or nuts.

Comanche children continue to practice the traditions of their ancestors.

A Comanche child is ready for a dance. Children learn about their tribe's traditions.

Chapter Five

Sharing the Traditions

The Comanche want their children
to know their traditions as well as those of
other Americans. The Comanche want
their children to succeed in modern
American life. Modern Comanche
leaders have taken steps to pass on
their culture. They continue to teach
traditional stories. They also take part
in community gatherings that show off
their Comanche traditions.

Each July, the Comanche gather at Walters, Oklahoma, for a weekend celebration of Comanche culture. The tradition is called the Comanche Homecoming. In 1952, the tradition began when the Comanche welcomed home their

During Comanche powwows, Comanche sing and drum.

soldiers from the Korean War. The Comanche held a victory dance, which became a yearly celebration.

Today, the homecoming includes dance competitions and a formal powwow with other Indians. Families return to Oklahoma from all over the United States to meet old friends, sing, drum, dance, and enjoy the music.

In September, the Comanche Nation Fair is held at Cache, Oklahoma. This event offers basketball, horseshoes, and other games. The festival also hosts an arts and crafts fair and a powwow with dance competitions. The Comanche are well known for their beadwork and powwow clothing called regalia.

Teaching the Language

The Comanche have worked to preserve their language and culture. Only a small number of Comanche can speak the language well. In July 1993, the Comanche Nation created the Comanche Language and Cultural

Preservation Committee. This group was charged with keeping the Comanche language alive.

The committee creates programs to teach young Comanche to speak, understand, and write their language. In 1994, the committee helped the nation adopt an official alphabet. The committee developed flash cards and a picture dictionary of the Comanche language. A Comanche reading book was created for use in schools and at summer language camps. In 1997, the committee developed a three-year language class for preschoolers in the school districts of Cache and Walters, Oklahoma. In 1999, the United Nations organization honored the committee for its efforts to preserve the Comanche language.

Though many Comanche now live far from their native plains, they celebrate their identity through powwows. They also celebrate with the tribal council and the Comanche language. They know that Comanche traditions and community are alive and well.

LaDonna Harris (1931-)

LaDonna Harris was born on a farm near Temple, Oklahoma, in 1931. Because her parents were separated and lived far away, Harris' grandparents raised her. Harris helped her grandparents with chores on their farm. She spoke only Comanche until she started school.

Harris met her future husband, Fred, in high school. They married in 1949. Fred Harris was elected to the Oklahoma State Senate and later the U.S. Senate. She helped with his campaign.

In Washington, D.C., Harris became friends with many politicians and their wives who were interested in fighting poverty and hate. In 1965, she was elected to lead Oklahomans for Indian Opportunity. This organization worked to solve problems of unemployment, poverty, and poor health among Oklahoma Indians.

In 1970, Harris created a group called Americans for Indian Opportunities. This group supports new programs of leadership for all American Indian tribes. The organization believes that the strength of American Indian communities is found in strong, independent tribal governments.

Comanche Timeline

Americans open the Santa Fe Trail from Missouri to New Mexico.

About 8,000 Comanche die from smallpox and cholera.

The Comanche, Kiowa, and Kiowa-Apache sign the Medicine Lodge Treaty. They move to a reservation in Indian Territory.

About 1700   **1821**   **1849–1851**   **1861–1865**   **1867**

The Comanche move onto the Great Plains.

The U.S. fights the Civil War.

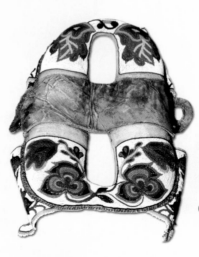

Comanche saddle

Buffalo hoof rattle

Quanah Parker surrenders his band of Comanche at Fort Sill.

Comanche men join the army to train as code talkers.

The Comanche adopt an alphabet.

1875   **1901–1906**   **1941**   **1967**   **1994**

The Comanche Nation adopts a new constitution.

Comanche Reservation breaks up after the General Allotment Act of 1887.

Glossary

allotment (uh-LOT-muhnt)—a small plot of land American Indians were allowed to keep after the U.S. government passed the General Allotment Act

nomad (NOH-mad)—a person who travels from place to place to find food and water

sinew (SIN-yoo)—a strong piece of body tissue that connects muscle to bone

travois (truh-VOY)—a simple vehicle made of two trailing poles and a platform or net to carry a load, usually pulled by a horse

vision quest (VIZH-uhn KWEST)—a four-day trip in which Comanche men hope to receive spiritual power

Internet Sites

Do you want to find out more about the Comanche?
Let FactHound, our fact-finding hound dog, do the research for you.

Here's how:

1) Visit *http://www.facthound.com*
2) Type in the **Book ID** number:
   0736821805
3) Click on **FETCH IT.**

FactHound will fetch Internet sites picked by our editors just for you!

Places to Write and Visit

Comanche Nation
P.O. Box 908
Lawton, OK 73502

Fort Sill National Historic Landmark
437 Quanah Road
Fort Sill, OK 73503-5100

Museum of the Great Plains
601 Northwest Ferris Avenue
Lawton, OK 73507

For Further Reading

Bial, Raymond. *The Comanche.* Lifeways. New York: Benchmark Books, 2000.

Gaines, Richard. *The Comanche.* Native Americans. Edina, Minn.: Abdo Publishers, 2000.

Streissguth, Thomas. *The Comanche.* Indigenous Peoples of North America. San Diego: Lucent Books, 2000.

Yacowitz, Caryn. *Comanche Indians.* Native Americans. Chicago: Heinemann Library, 2002.

Index